The Together Book

written by
Revena Dwight

illustrated by
Roger Bradfield

🌷 A GOLDEN BOOK • NEW YORK

Visit us on the Web!
randomhousekids.com
SesameStreetBooks.com
www.sesamestreet.org
Educators and librarians, for a variety of teaching tools, visit us at RHTeachersLibrarians.com
ISBN 978-1-5247-1978-4 (trade) — ISBN 978-1-5247-1979-1 (ebook)
Printed in the United States of America
10 9 8 7 6 5 4 3

What do I have that needs a helper?
I have a wagon that just won't go. . . .

Who has something good for wagons?

WHEELS ARE THE NIFTIEST
THINGS I KNOW!

What do I have that needs a helper?
I have a double-thick malted milk. . . .

Who has something good for drinking?

DOWN IT GOES, AS SMOOTH AS SILK.

What do I have that needs a helper?
I have a hill piled high with snow. . . .

Who has something good for sliding?

ONE, TWO, THREE—
AND DOWN WE GO!

What do I have that needs a helper?
I have a cake that's going to fall. . . .

Who can keep the cake from falling?

LET'S SIT DOWN AND EAT IT ALL!

What do I have that needs a helper?
I have skates that won't stay tight. . . .

Who has something to make them fit me?

GOOD! NOW LOOK!
THEY FIT JUST RIGHT!

Every day I need a helper.
Every day you need one, too.
There's so much we can do together. . . .

YOU HELP ME, AND I'LL HELP YOU!